W9-BWU-435

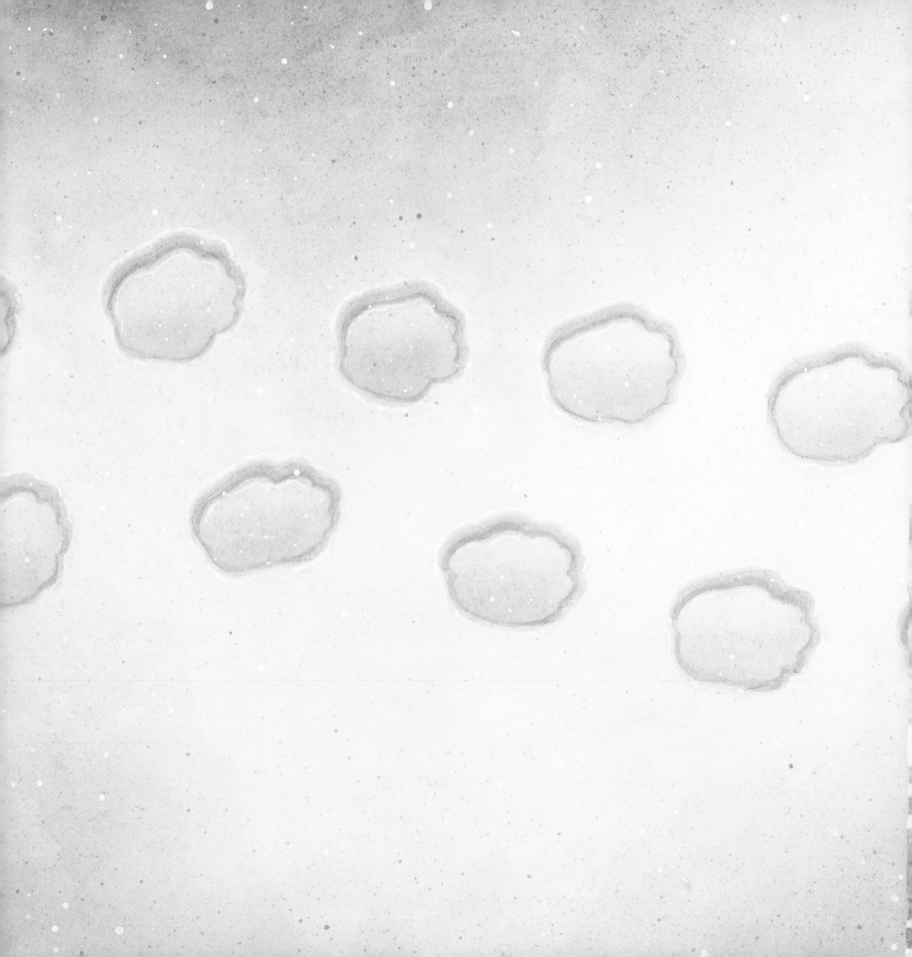

A VERY
FIONA CHRISTMAS

NEW YORK TIMES BESTSELLING ILLUSTRATOR
RICHARD COWDREY

ZONDERkidz

To Deborah.
For being first to recognize a great story,
a tale of perseverance, strength of heart, and love ...
and then to share her love with the rest of us.

–RC

ZONDERKIDZ

A Very Fiona Christmas
Copyright © 2019 by Zondervan
Illustrations © 2019 by Zondervan

Requests for information
should be addressed to:

Zonderkidz, 3900 Sparks Dr. SE,
Grand Rapids, Michigan 49546

Library of Congress Cataloging-in-Publication Data
Names: Cowdrey, Richard, illustrator.
Title: A very Fiona Christmas / illustrated by Richard Cowdrey.
Description: Grand Rapids, Michigan : Zonderkidz, [2019] | Summary: Fiona the
    baby hippo is puzzled by the excitement the other zoo animals feel over
    Christmas, but after meeting Chloe the koala, who has just arrived, she
    begins to understand. |
Identifiers: LCCN 2019007025 (print) | LCCN 2019010228 (ebook) | ISBN
    9780310767718 () | ISBN 9780310767732 (hardcover)
Subjects: | CYAC: Hippopotamus--Fiction. | Animals--Infancy--Fiction. | Zoo
    animals--Fiction. | Christmas--Fiction.
Classification: LCC PZ7.1.C685 (ebook) | LCC PZ7.1.C685 Ver 2019 (print) |
    DDC [E]--dc23
LC record available at https://lccn.loc.gov/2019007025

Illustrated by: Richard Cowdrey
Contributors: Barbara Herndon and Mary Hassinger
Art direction and design: Cindy Davis and Kris Nelson

Printed in China

19 20 21 22 23 24 25 /DSC/ 20 19 18 17 16 15 14 13 12 11 10 9 8 7 6 5 4 3 2 1

It was a cold winter's day and the zoo was buzzing with excitement.
Fiona bundled up in her favorite scarf, kissed her mama goodbye,
and set out to see what all the commotion was about.

Fiona listened to her friends talking.
She wondered why they were so excited.
This was her first Christmas at the zoo,
and she still had a lot to learn.

"Christmas?" she asked.
"What's Christmas?"

"Come with us, Fiona!
We'll show you!"

And so Fiona went ...

Fiona played in snow for the very first time.
She slipped and slid down the snowy
hill with her penguin pals.
She wiggled and giggled right
along with them, until ...

OPENING SOON!
KOALA-TOWN

Fiona found herself surrounded by snow animals!
She smiled and felt a little warm inside even as she stood in the cold snow.

As she nuzzled her scarf to keep warm, she let out a snort, wiggled her ears, and asked,

"Is THIS Christmas?"

"Come see more!" rumbled polar bear. He lumbered off toward the big, tall, bright, and colorful ...

Christmas Tree!!!

"It's beautiful!"

Fiona shouted with glee.
She looked up at the star on the top.
It was shining brightly against
the late afternoon sky.

Fiona felt a little twinkly inside as she hung her very own ornament on the tree.
As Fiona gazed in wonder, she let out a snort, wiggled her ears, and asked,
"Is THIS Christmas?"

Fiona heard jingling bells and everywhere she looked she saw sparkling lights and glittery decorations.

She met some reindeer.

Fiona even found mistletoe!

Fiona felt all tingly inside. Then she let out a snort, wiggled her ears, and asked,

"Is THIS Christmas?"

Fiona was getting hungry.
She was getting cold too.

It was time to get back to Hippo Cove
for lettuce and squash
and a snuggle with Mama.

Back at home, Fiona quietly munched and crunched her dinner.
Mama wondered why she wasn't her usual playful little hippo.

"What's Christmas, Mama?"

Fiona asked. "My friends showed me lots of things today,
but I still don't know what it is."

"Tomorrow is Christmas day, Fiona. Spend time with your friends.
See how happy they are. You'll get this, Fiona.
You will feel it in your heart."

ROAR HONK HONK COOOOO COOOO

Squeak Squeak

Chirp Chirp Chirp Chirp

Grooowl

Fiona was awake early on Christmas morning.
From far away she could hear the animals
calling and cooing and roaring.
The whole zoo seemed
noisier than ever before!

Squawk

Purrrrrr

Squeak Squeak

As Fiona set out in search of Christmas,
she noticed a furry little animal sitting on a signpost.
She looked a little sad and very chilly.

Fiona slid close. "Hi, I'm Fiona," she said.
"You must be new."

"I'm Chloe,"
the little koala whispered softly.

As the new friends
smiled at each other,
the ground began to shake.
Icicles tinkled, lights twinkled,
and a stampede
of animals whizzed by!

"It's
Christmas!"

"Time for presents!"

The animals raced to their stockings.
They were filled with apples and oranges,
lettuce leaves, and worms.
There were bouncy balls and colorful things to chew.

There was even a stocking for Fiona—
with her name written in sparkling glitter.
But there wasn't one for Chloe ...

"You didn't see a stocking with my name on it, did you, Fiona?"
Chloe asked as she shivered in the snow.
"No, I didn't," said Fiona.

Fiona's chunky chins rubbed against her soft, tattered scarf—
the one Mama helped wrap around her neck to keep her warm.

It was in that moment that Fiona finally understood.
Christmas is friends and fun and snow and lights and trees...
AND LOVE!

As she slipped her favorite scarf over the little koala's shoulders,
Fiona let out a snort, wiggled her ears, and said,
"THIS is Christmas!"

"Merry Christmas, Chloe."

"Merry Christmas, Fiona."

"Hey, everyone! Come meet Chloe.
She just moved here!"
Fiona called out to her friends.

"It's nice
to
meet you!"

That night, Fiona shook snowflakes off as she returned to Hippo Cove, ready for dinner.

"Merry Christmas, my chilly little hippo," said Mama.
"Where's your scarf?"

Fiona smiled as she gave Mama a quick Christmas nuzzle.
"I gave it to my new friend. She needed it more than me."
"You make me very proud," said Mama.

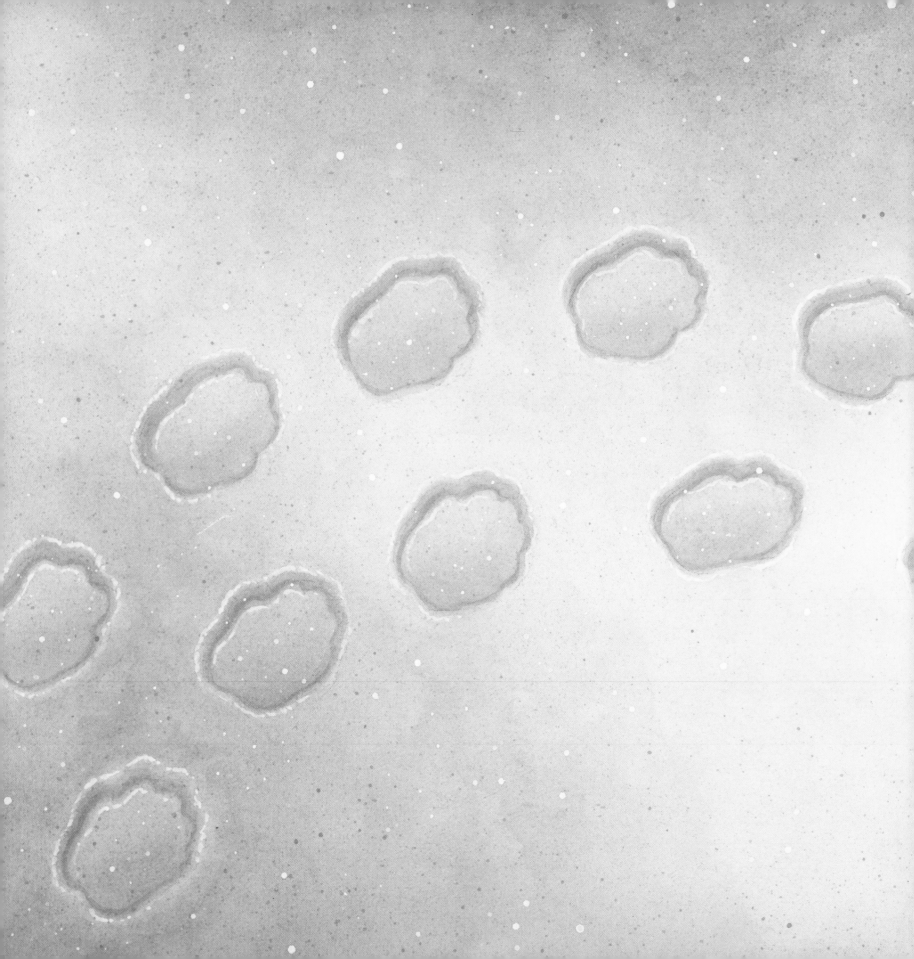